For Rose

With sincere thanks to Lucy Brownridge
and Karissa Santos.

Gold Rush © 2024 Quarto Publishing plc.
Text © 2024 Flora Delargy.
Illustrations © 2024 Flora Delargy.

First Published in 2024 by Wide Eyed Editions,
an imprint of The Quarto Group.
100 Cummings Center, Suite 265D, Beverly, MA 01915, USA.
T (978) 282-9590 F (978) 283-2742 **www.Quarto.com**

The right of Flora Delargy to be identified as the illustrator and author of this
work has been asserted by them in accordance with the Copyright, Designs and
Patents Act, 1988 (United Kingdom).

A CIP record for this book is available from the Library of Congress.

ISBN 978-0-7112-6389-5
E-ISBN 978-0-7112-6388-8
The illustrations were created using ink and watercolour
Set in Bookeyed Jack, Vincente and Quasimoda

Production Controller: Dawn Cameron
Editorial Director: Lucy Brownridge
Art Director: Karissa Santos
Publisher: Georgia Buckthorn and Debbie Foy

Manufactured in Guangdong, China TT072024

9 8 7 6 5 4 3 2 1

GOLD RUSH

WIDE EYED EDITIONS

Kate Carmack (Shaaw Tláa)

CONTENTS

Klondike, Yukon Territory — 9

The Yukon's First Nations — 10

16th August 1896, Bonanza Creek, Yukon Territory — 12

KATE CARMACK (Shaaw Tláa): The Discoverer — 14

News Spreads to Seattle — 16

The Eternal Allure of Gold — 18

MARTHA BLACK: The Stateswoman — 21

Martha Joins the Trail — 22

Supplies for the Journey — 24

Routes to the Gold Fields — 26

Trekking the Chilkoot Trail — 28

Chilkoot Golden Staircase — 30

Riding the Rapids to Dawson City — 32

BELINDA MULROONEY: The Boomtown Entrepreneur — 34

Belinda Arrives in Dawson — 36

Beyond Traditional Roles — 38

Building a City from Scratch — 40

The Fairview Hotel — 42

George Carmack

Bessie Couture

Nero

NELLIE CASHMAN: The Prospector   44

    The Miner's Angel   *46*

    Methods of Mining   *48*

    Mining the Earth   *50*

    Pioneering Change   *52*

    Nellie Hits the Bonanza   *54*

THE BEAUTY OF THE NORTH   56

    The Strike Moves On   *58*

    Martha Devotes her Life to the Yukon   *61*

    Nellie and Belinda Give Back to the Community   *62*

    Devastation of the Way of Life   *65*

THE IMPACT OF KATE CARMACK   67

    Discrimination and Injustice   *68*

    Kate and the Spirit of the Frontier   *70*

    Canadian Mining Hall of Fame   *72*

Glossary   *74*

Chief Isaac

Nellie Cashman

Martha Black

Belinda Mulrooney

ARCTIC
OCEAN

UNITED STATES
ALASKA

YUKON

PACIFIC
OCEAN

CANADA

NUNAVUT

NORTHWEST
TERRITORIES

HUDSON
BAY

BRITISH
COLUMBIA

ALBERTA

SASKATCH-
EWAN

MANITOBA

KLONDIKE, YUKON TERRITORY

Stretching from the border of British Columbia to the frozen waters of the Arctic Ocean, the remote Yukon Territory in North West Canada spans thousands of miles. It's a beautiful but dangerous wilderness, with glaciers and endless open spaces surrounded by rugged mountain ranges.

Flowing through the region is the mighty Yukon river. Its name is believed to have originated from the Gwich'in word 'Yu-kun-ah' meaning "great river." It runs through the Yukon, across Alaska, and into the Bering Sea. At over 2,000 miles long, it is also sprinkled with gold.

When the gold was first found, it sparked a huge search in the area. It changed the landscape and the people, in an event which became known as the Klondike Gold Rush.

The Yukon's First Nations

The original inhabitants of the Yukon, the First Nations, had learnt over centuries how to survive. They moved with the changing seasons along rivers and in the woodlands, fishing and gathering, hunting and trapping. However to outsiders, the region was inhospitable with short summers and long dark winters, temperatures sometimes dipping as low as -58°F.

There are 14 First Nations in the Yukon and they are each organized into two moieties or clans: The Wolf and the Crow. A Crow is only permitted to marry a Wolf, and vice versa. Their children are born into the clan of their mother.

The clans have responsibilities to each other that help maintain peaceful and prosperous relationships within the communities. In total there are eight language groups spoken by First Nations: Gwich'in, Hän, Kaska, Upper Tanana, Northern Tutchone, Southern Tutchone, Tagish, and Tlingit.

As the land was colonized and the first outsiders and fur traders entered the region, life for the First Nations communities began to change. The newcomers spread their beliefs and practices, but they also introduced diseases such as smallpox and measles, which had devastating impacts on First Nation peoples.

August 16 1896, Bonanza Creek, Yukon Territory

Shaaw Tláa belonged to the First Nation Tagish and Tlingit peoples. Her name meant "Older than Old." Shaaw's mother was a member of the Tagish Wolf clan and her father was head of the Tlingit Crow clan. Her community moved within an area encompassing four large lakes: Tagish, Bennett, Nares, and Marsh. It was common for indigenous people to also have a European name, whether by choice or given to them by the newcomers who struggled with First Nation languages.

Shaaw was resourceful and had a deep respect and understanding of the Yukon. She knew what plants could be used for medicines, which could be eaten, and which to avoid. She knew how to catch salmon with traps on the river and hunt rabbits in the woodland. She tanned hides, sewed mittens, and made moccasins.

In the summer of 1896, Kate, as she was now known following her marriage, had been traveling with her husband, a white American prospector called George Carmack. Accompanying them was her brother Keish (Skookum Jim Mason), and nephew Káa Goox (Dawson Charlie).

Along one of the Yukon river's many winding tributaries this small group of travelers had set up camp in the traditional territory of the Tr'ondëk Hwëch'in First Nation, who hunted and gathered there for generations.

But this party of four were searching for more than just fish and game...

13

KATE CARMACK (SHAAW TLÁA)
The Discoverer

And it was Kate who found the gold.

This account, however, is only one of many versions of the discovery of the gold strike. As the white settler colonies were established, the rights and opportunities for the indigenous people of the Yukon were taken away. Some say it was Keish who spotted the gold while others say it was George Carmack who made the discovery. It was decided the find should be registered in George's name because other miners might not accept a claim lodged by First Nations people.

News Spreads to Seattle

News of the gold strike at Bonanza Creek tore across the Yukon territory. Prospectors in the area dropped what they were doing and headed off in pursuit of the precious metal. Hopefuls arrived in their dozens, up and down the creek, digging feverishly to extract the glittering treasure from the hard, frozen ground.

By July of 1897, steamships carried successful prospectors who had set out with nothing and returned rich beyond their wildest dreams to San Francisco and Seattle.

The word was out. Within a few hours of the arrival of the first Klondike miners, many folk walked out of their jobs and began planning their journey northwards. As gold fever spread around the world, tens of thousands joined them, crossing oceans and continents in pursuit of riches.

The Eternal Allure of Gold

Human fascination with gold goes back far into the mists of time. Although it is found deep in the dark bedrock, its warm glow is like that of the sun. Its beauty, malleability, and near indestructibility has linked it to immortality and it has often been prized above all other metals in history. The first artefacts made from the precious metal were produced over six thousand years ago and since that time gold has been fashioned into jewelry, plates, goblets, statues, and religious objects.

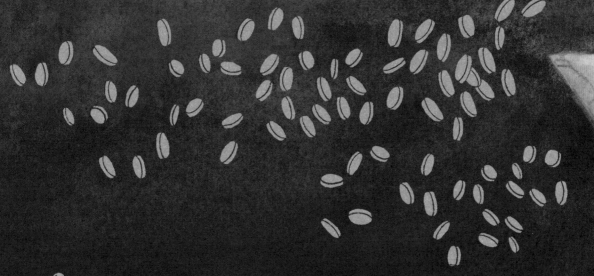

The Gold Standard

A great part of its appeal is that it is seen as a store of value. The first gold coins were produced two and half thousand years ago. Even when they were replaced with banknotes, confidence in paper money depended on its ready conversion to gold.

The ancient Egyptians were entranced by gold. The tomb of the young Pharaoh Tutankhamun constructed in the 14th century BCE contained incredible amounts of the metal, with the inner most coffin itself made of over 240lb of solid gold.

Gold was associated with wealth, success and spirituality, and the story of how it was found was often just as powerful as its value. One woman who longed to begin a new chapter in her own story was preparing to set sail from Seattle...

MARTHA BLACK
The Stateswoman

Martha Joins the Trail

Kate Carmack may have unearthed the first gold but the Seattle Post-Intelligencer newspaper saw fit to run the headline 'NO PLACE FOR WOMEN' in March 1898, proclaiming that women were "utterly unfit" for life on the trail. 31-year-old Martha Black was just one of a number of fearless women who paid no attention to this. She longed for the thrill of adventure.

Martha felt restless and unhappy with domestic life. As her husband, Will, and friend Eli discussed their impending trip to the gold fields, she felt a great desire to play her part in it. With their sons settled in boarding school, it was decided she would accompany Will and her brother George to the gold fields.

Just before the party were due to travel, Will changed his mind and suggested they remain in Chicago. Martha didn't agree. She wrote to Will telling him she would continue on without him. "I could not turn back now," she thought. "This was my destiny!"

Supplies for the Journey

The Canadian Mounted Police declared that each miner must bring a year's worth of food to ensure self-sufficiency in the harsh climate. Almost overnight, the streets of Seattle were crowded with stores offering an astonishing array of supplies and many struggled to keep up with the incredible demand.

Travelers were advised to gather a vast array of items:

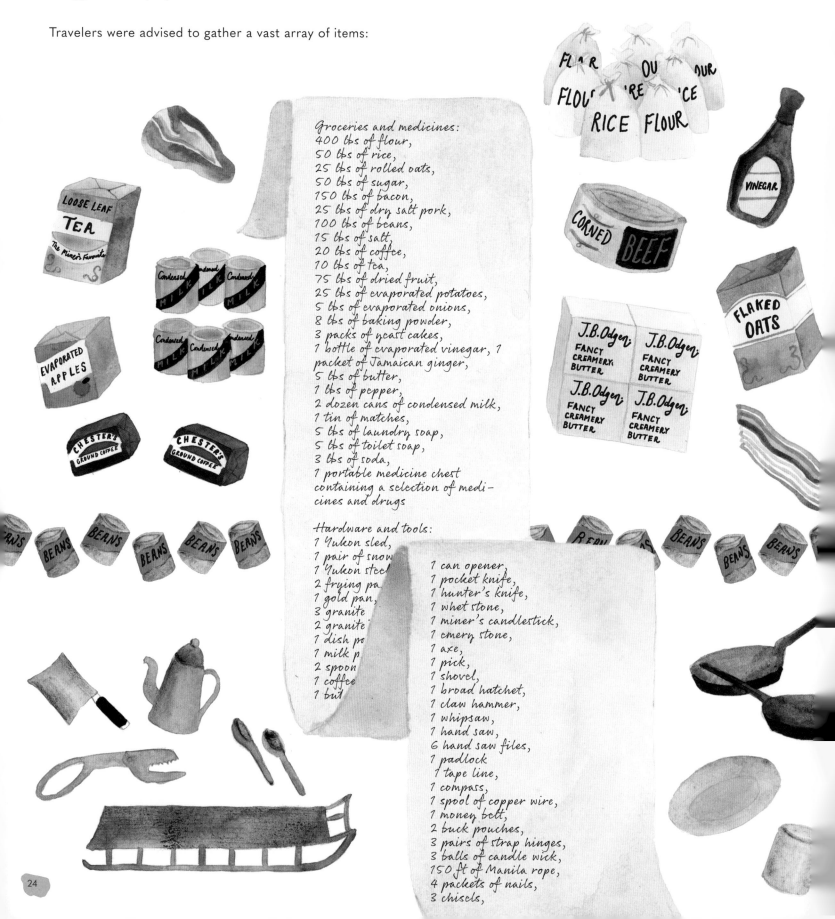

Groceries and medicines:
400 lbs of flour,
50 lbs of rice,
25 lbs of rolled oats,
50 lbs of sugar,
150 lbs of bacon,
25 lbs of dry salt pork,
100 lbs of beans,
15 lbs of salt,
20 lbs of coffee,
10 lbs of tea,
75 lbs of dried fruit,
25 lbs of evaporated potatoes,
5 lbs of evaporated onions,
8 lbs of baking powder,
3 packs of yeast cakes,
1 bottle of evaporated vinegar, 1 packet of Jamaican ginger,
5 lbs of butter,
1 lbs of pepper,
2 dozen cans of condensed milk,
1 tin of matches,
5 lbs of laundry soap,
5 lbs of toilet soap,
3 lbs of soda,
1 portable medicine chest containing a selection of medi-cines and drugs

Hardware and tools:
1 Yukon sled,
1 pair of snow
1 Yukon steel
2 frying pa
1 gold pan,
3 granite
2 granite
1 dish po
1 milk p
2 spoon
1 coffee
1 but

1 can opener,
1 pocket knife,
1 hunter's knife,
1 whet stone,
1 miner's candlestick,
1 emery stone,
1 axe,
1 pick,
1 shovel,
1 broad hatchet,
1 claw hammer,
1 whipsaw,
1 hand saw,
6 hand saw files,
1 padlock
1 tape line,
1 compass,
1 spool of copper wire,
1 money belt,
2 buck pouches,
3 pairs of strap hinges,
3 balls of candle wick,
150 ft of Manila rope,
4 packets of nails,
3 chisels,

1 rip saw,
1 man saw

Clothing:
mackinaw suit,
heavy canvas suit,
oil skin suit,
heavy wool shirt,
lighter wool shirt,
heavy wool
underwear,
Heavy blankets,
broad-brimmed hat,
4 pairs of woolen mitts,
silk muffler, sweater,
pair of rubber gloves,
high-top leather boots,
rubber boots,
felt shoes
Arctic shoes,
a dozen pairs of mixed socks,
sleeping bag,
4 pairs of towels

Routes to the Gold Fields

There were a number of different routes to the Klondike and none were straightforward. Most, like Martha, started out from port cities such as Seattle. They boarded ships and headed north to the Alaskan ports of Skagway and Dyea.

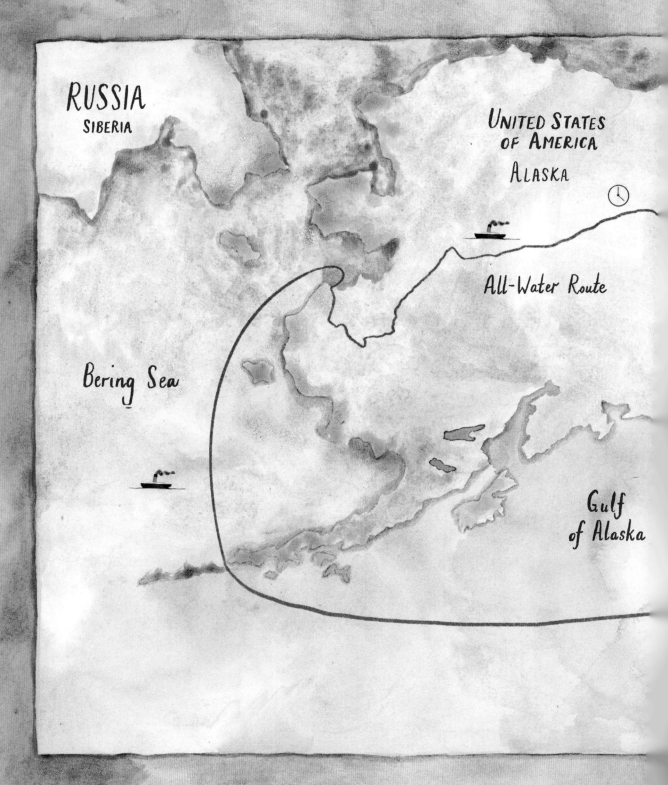

RUSSIA
SIBERIA

UNITED STATES
OF AMERICA
ALASKA

All-Water Route

Bering Sea

Gulf
of Alaska

From Skagway, stampeders took the White Pass Trail, a passage following the Skagway River. The path was treacherous and horses and donkeys easily broke their legs. The trail earned itself the nickname "Dead Horse Trail."

The most famous route was
the Chilkoot Trail. The route
was wider for trekking but the
final slope was perilous

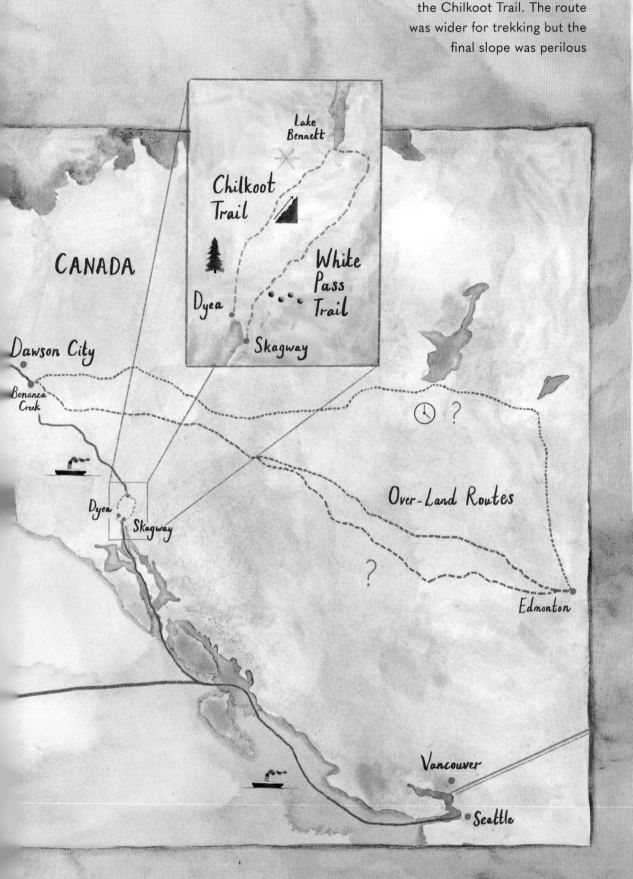

water route

wood and forestland

steep gradient

risk of blizzard

potholes

slow route

? unpredictable

------ by path

——— by water

CANADA

Lake Bennett

Chilkoot Trail

White Pass Trail

Dyea

Skagway

Dawson City

Bonanza Creek

Dyea

Skagway

Over-Land Routes

Edmonton

Vancouver

Seattle

There were two other less popular routes. The All-Water Route was a steamboat
ride of over 4,000 miles from Seattle to St Michael and then on to Dawson City.
It was slow and expensive. Lastly, the overland routes, from Edmonton, were
perhaps the most impractical. A journey of at least 1,500 miles through a network
of poorly defined trails faced stampeders who chose this path.

Trekking the Chilkoot Trail

Martha chose the Chilkoot Trail. The journey north from Seattle, via the port town of Dyea, to the gold fields was 1,500 kilometres long.

It involved hauling equipment over mountain passes where the winter temperature fell as low as -58°F.

The Chilkoot Trail had traditionally been overseen by the Tlingit people, who had been using it as a trade passage for hundreds of years. When the outsiders arrived the Tlingit used their position to establish a profitable packing business. However, as the numbers using the pass grew, they were forced to share the work with other groups.

Most stampeders wildly underestimated the challenges ahead. The trail began as a peaceful walk through forestland and meadow—but Martha soon found the route steepening and the increasingly rocky path gathered a coating of snow and ice. The most difficult passages of the trail still lay ahead...

Chilkoot Golden Staircase

From the base at Sheep Camp to the summit of the Chilkoot pass was a mere four miles but the last stage required stampeders climb 1,500 steps at a challenging 35 degree incline—a similar gradient to household stairs!

Many of the women on the journey still wore the clothing of the day: restrictive corsets made with animal bone, long skirts, tailored jackets, lightweight shoes. Although most of them did not carry their own heavy packs, this attire was still completely unsuitable for the trek. Hitching up her long skirts, Martha would, without doubt, have thought how useful a pair of trousers would have been!

Stampeders poured into Sheep
Camp and all through the winter an
endless stream of hopefuls slowly
ascended this "Golden Staircase."

Riding the Rapids to Dawson City

Once they had reached the summit, the stampeders passed through the Canadian Mounties' Customs Check Point and descended to Lake Lindemann. Martha rode the rapids down the rough waters in a small boat, the spray of the water so thick it obscured the shore. The exhilarating twists and turns of the great Yukon river took her breath away.

Exhausted but triumphant, she had arrived at Dawson City!

Of the 100,000 stampeders who set out for the gold fields, around 70,000 either turned back or perished. A sea of white tents and temporary buildings greeted Martha as her boat was pulled ashore.

Founded in 1897, Dawson was a true boom town with a population of 17,000 at the peak of the gold rush. With no sanitation, a food shortage, and tens of thousands hoping to make a quick million, it would take grit and determination to be a success in this town...

BELINDA MULROONEY & NERO

The Boomtown Entrepreneur

And few had more grit than Belinda.

Belinda Prepares to Depart for Dawson

25-year-old Irish-born Belinda Mulrooney was already in Canada when she caught wind of the strike at Bonanza Creek. She and her family had moved to Pennsylvania from County Sligo when she was a child. Belinda was smart and resourceful and by her early twenties had become an entrepreneur, having run a general store in the Alaskan city of Juneau and bought and sold a business at the Chicago World Fair of 1893.

HARDWARE & TOOLS

ALASKA SUPPLIES

SEATTLE

Belinda shrewdly realized that rather than mining for gold, she could make more money selling goods to miners. In 1896 she traveled to Seattle to purchase her Yukon outfit, discarding her corset for a boned skirt, thick shirt, and a fur hooded parka. She set off in April 1897 for the gold fields at Bonanza Creek with her year's supplies and plenty of merchandise to sell in Dawson, where she soon became recognized along with her faithful canine companion, Nero the St. Bernard. To help transport her goods, she hired a large party but insisted on pulling along her share of the load.

Beyond Traditional Roles

Although it was reportedly **"No Place for Women,"** those who made it to the boom towns arrived exhausted, craving the kind of domestic comfort that women of the time were expected to provide.

For some entrepreneurial women, the constant stream of hungry and weary stampeders seeking respite from the trail presented a golden opportunity.

Success didn't only mean hitting a gold strike in the hills. In the Alaskan port town of Skagway, women such as Bessie Couture thrived despite the town's unsafe and anarchic reputation.

GOLD DUST BOUGHT & SOLD HERE!

THE

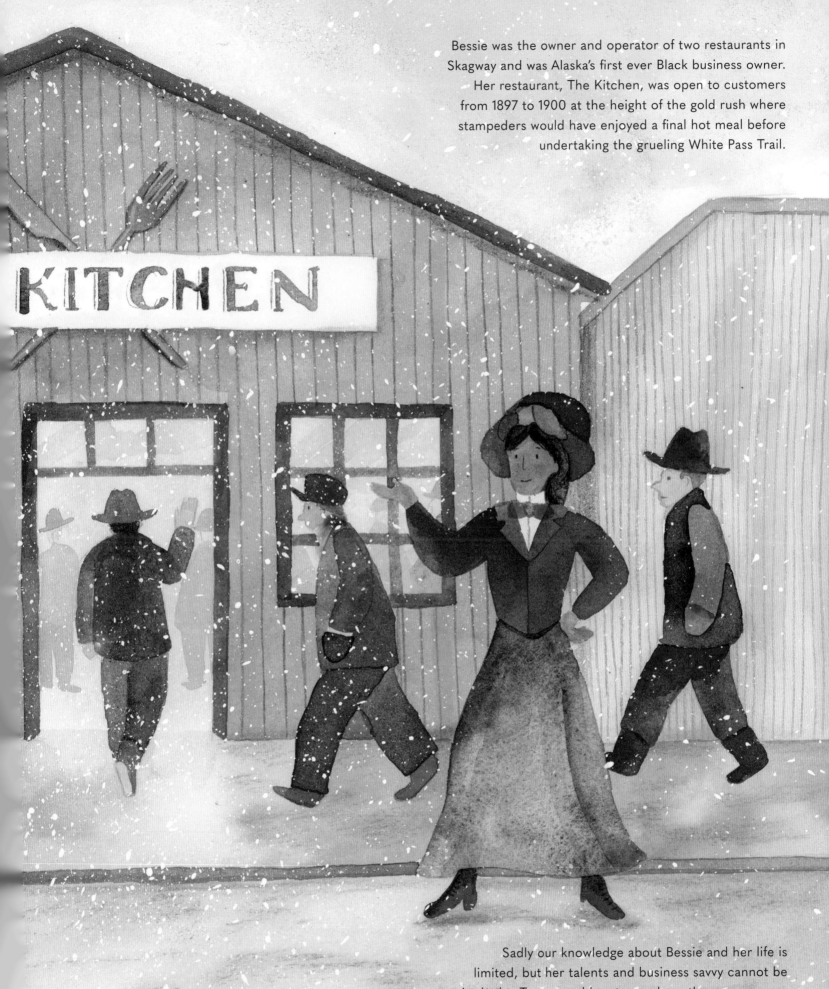

Bessie was the owner and operator of two restaurants in Skagway and was Alaska's first ever Black business owner. Her restaurant, The Kitchen, was open to customers from 1897 to 1900 at the height of the gold rush where stampeders would have enjoyed a final hot meal before undertaking the grueling White Pass Trail.

KITCHEN

Sadly our knowledge about Bessie and her life is limited, but her talents and business savvy cannot be in doubt. To succeed in a town where there were many lawless people and ruthless opportunists shows true determination and resilience.

Building a City from Scratch

As soon as she arrived in Dawson, Belinda Mulrooney's supplies of luxury items such as silk, cotton and hot water bottles were snapped up by stampeders at a profit of six times the cost. Belinda had resolved that if she couldn't go prospecting in the hills or rivers, she'd earn her gold dust another way.

Using the proceeds, Belinda set up a store, and soon after opened a restaurant and eventually bought up a block of properties on Front Street. The settlement turned from a ramshackle assortment of tents to the major city of Dawson. The town was filled with stampeders eager to spend their hard-earned gold dust in the many bars and restaurants, where the sparkling substance was legal tender.

Belinda was determined to be near the mines and, to the amusement of the men who felt Dawson was the only place for a hotel, Belinda opened her first roadhouse 15 miles away, near the gold fields at Bonanza Creek. The hotel was a huge success and provided a convenient spot for miners to meet and conduct business.

The Fairview Hotel

Belinda wasn't content to stop there. She was determined to get her cut of the gold flowing through Dawson. She decided to build the grandest, most opulent hotel in the city. The Fairview would rival the best that Portland, Seattle, or San Francisco had to offer, she thought to her herself. Belinda used every ounce of her ingenuity to source supplies and building materials. She overcame obstacles at every turn, from shortages of lumber to the challenge of transporting the furnishings over the White Pass herself.

In July 1898, the Fairview Hotel opened on Front Street in Dawson. Many had bet large sums of money that Belinda wouldn't have the resources or know-how to complete the project, but she proved them all wrong! Her hotel boasted cut glass chandeliers, tables set with silver and linen, and bedrooms equipped with brass bedsteads.

The Seattle Post-Intelligencer may have written that the goldfields were "**No Place for Women**," but Belinda had become one of the true legends of the Klondike Gold Rush.

NELLIE CASHMAN
The Prospector

Meanwhile, another legend was preparing to tackle the trail.

The Miner's Angel

At the time of Kate's discovery, Nellie Cashman had over 25 years' experience as a prospector of precious metals. She had emigrated from Ireland with her family around 1850, at the time of the potato famine, and spent her life running boarding houses and working mining claims. Her work took her from the frozen frontiers of Cassiar, British Columbia to the toughest desert towns of Arizona.

Nellie left the Cassiar in 1879 and traveled to Tuscon, Arizona where she opened a restaurant. She often let struggling miners eat for free. She then moved onto the silver boom town of Tombstone, one of the most dangerous and lawless towns in the United States.

Not only did Nellie prove the gold fields were places for women, the Rush also presented an opportunity for her to help those who needed it most. In 1874, she led a mission to rescue miners trapped in a blizzard and suffering from scurvy. She hauled supplies of fruit and vegetables, which she had paid for herself, for the men, and the journey took 77 days. Along with countless donations to help build churches and hospitals, Nellie earned herself the nickname "Angel of the Cassiar."

The fifty-four year old wasted no time in organizing an expedition to the Klondike when she heard the news of the discovery. "This is my chance to make a million or two," she thought to herself.

Methods of Mining

The journey to the goldfields was long and arduous, but the stampeders' hard work was just beginning. The creeks and hills surrounding Dawson were said to be overflowing with gold but how could it be extracted?

Gold is a heavy substance and often settles where the gravel meets bedrock.

The simplest method of extracting gold was called "panning." Prospectors would collect gravel or sand at the creeks and swirl the water and gravel/sand mixture around a circular pan.

This motion would allow the lighter pebbles and rocks to spill out, leaving the heavier gold particles to collect at the bottom.

One of the most important and innovative inventions was the sluice box system. It consisted of long narrow wooden boxes with barriers placed along the bottom called "riffles." The boxes were linked together in downward incline and water and paydirt would be poured through. The wooden riffles caught the heavy gold as it fell to the bottom of the boxes and the lighter elements flowed out.

Mining the Earth

In order to extract large quantities of pay dirt in the long winter months, miners would have to break through layers of permafrost to reach the gravel bedrock beneath.

In order to thaw the ground, miners dug down into the earth with picks and shovels and lit fires within these shafts. The shafts were 4 by 6 feet wide to allow a person and bucket to pass up and down by a rope and pulley system. Most mines reached down over 30 feet below the surface.

frozen mud

frozen gravel

Once they had reached the bedrock, miners would begin to dig horizontally. This was called "drifting" and allowed miners to gather as much gravel containing the gold dust and nuggets as possible.

gold-rich bedrock

It was dangerous work. Miners were at risk of inhaling toxic levels of smoke with potential to cause sight loss or even suffocation. Although permafrost held the ceilings of the shafts in place, sometimes the earth caved in on top of those working at the bottom. Over five tons of gold were pulled out of the earth around Dawson in 1897.

Pioneering Change

Many women like Nellie were keen to mine for gold and compete with the men but faced discriminatory obstacles as single women. Gold mining was seen as taxing work and most believed that there were jobs more suited to women such as cooking, cleaning, or teaching. Additionally, polite society frowned on unmarried women staking claims.

Despite these obstacles, Nellie was highly successful in her ventures. She ran five separate boarding houses in Dawson which proved useful, not just as a way of funding her mining claims, but also as a way of picking up stories and leads from her mining customers. Nellie earned the respect and admiration of miners through her generosity to those who were down on their luck.

She was admired as one of the very few women to work her own mine. It was back-breaking and grubby work but Nellie was a seasoned prospector and knew how to handle herself.

Nellie hits the Bonanza

With her Mine no.19, Nellie's hard work paid off, and she struck the big time! The mine yielded an incredible $100,000 or $3m in today's money.

THE BEAUTY OF THE NORTH

The Strike Moves On

For the stampeders who made it to the Klondike,
the crushing reality for many was that the amount of
gold that existed in the region was completely out of
proportion with the scale of the stampede.

The Rush brought out the very best and very worst
of the stampeders who braved the trails, and for most
the dream of gold remained just that. After just a
few short years, on July 27 1899, gold was found on
the beach at Nome in Alaska, and by August
the first exodus of 8,000 left Dawson for Nome.

Almost as quickly as it had begun, the Klondike
Gold Rush had ended.

Dawson City went from a bustling community
of 17,000 at the height of the Gold Rush, to a
population of just 8,000 in the years after.

The mountains and creeks surrounding Dawson, which had been full of the sounds of industry, suddenly became quiet again.

Martha Devotes her Life to the Yukon

Martha Black had fallen in love with the region and spent her days running a sawmill and quartz mill on the Yukon river. Although life in the Klondike was a profound change for her, Martha was fascinated by the extremes of weather. The summers were warm and the nights so light, and yet the winter nights grew darker and darker as the months stretched on. She was captivated by the shimmering Northern Lights dancing in the sky above her.

In spring, Martha watched as the hills bloomed with spring flowers. She was fascinated with the vibrant plant life and began documenting the varieties that she found. She loved the yellow water crowfoot trailing along the edge of the streams and the beautiful white blossoms of the anemone. Martha lived out the rest of her life in the Yukon and eventually became the first woman from Northern Canada elected to the House of Commons in Ottawa.

Nellie and Belinda Give Back to the Community

For Nellie, chasing gold meant more than just profit. Her earnings allowed her to give back to the community she lived in. She worked alongside Jesuit Priest Fr William Judge to improve the living conditions of the residents of Dawson, where poor sanitation and extreme weather led to outbreaks of flu and scurvy. Nellie's fundraising made it possible for the construction of a three-storey addition to St Mary's Hospital.

or Belinda, chasing gold gave her the chance to establish herself as powerful entrepreneur and help play a part in taking Dawson from amshackle town to a vibrant and thriving city. She helped Dawson get a elephone and water company, which brought safe drinking water to the esidents. Even though she fell on hard times later in life, she built back er fortune in the Fairbanks gold fields through sheer tenacity.

Devastation of the Way of Life

The frenzy of the gold rush years left many casualties. The First
Nation communities of the Yukon suffered greatly as a result of
the influx of stampeders. Their ancient hunting and fishing grounds
were destroyed by the mining industry and they were forced to move
away from the land they had lived on for hundreds of years.

The leader of the Hän, Chief Isaac, played a crucial diplomatic role in
protecting his people from the newcomers to the region and worked with the
Canadian government and the Anglican Church to resettle the community 3
down the Yukon river at Moosehide. Chief Isaac recognized the risk that the Hän
culture could be lost through the impact of the settlers and took steps to entrust
the people's songs and dances to First Nations communities living in Alaska for
safekeeping.

The new residents also brought new diseases with them which the First Nation
communities had no defense against. Their customs and way of life were at risk
of being lost forever. As the years passed, the community fought back and by
the late twentieth century the actions of the settlers during the gold rush years
and beyond were recognized as human rights violations. Little by little, the
community began to reclaim the land and took back control of their
heritage. The descendants of the Hän people, who lived along the
Yukon River for millennia, now call themselves Tr'ondëk Hwëch'in—
the people of the Klondike River—and account for a third of
residents in Dawson.

THE IMPACT OF KATE CARMACK

Discrimination and Injustice

Kate's involvement in the discovery of gold at Bonanza Creek
should have ensured her a comfortable and secure future with
her husband George Carmack and their daughter Graphie.
Unfortunately this was not to be.

After claiming their windfall, Kate and George traveled to various cities in the US including Seattle and San Francisco. Their marriage disintegrated after just a few short years, with George maintaining their Tagish marriage had never been lawful. Out of place and far from home, Kate struggled to adapt to life in places that weren't welcoming of her culture. And after her legal battle to secure custody of her daughter was unsuccessful, she returned home, discovering that her Tagish village had been displaced by the Yukon and White Pass Railway.

Kate suffered discrimination on two counts: for being part of a First Nation community and also for being a woman. She also could not read or write so we don't know how she felt about her role in the discovery of gold but we can certainly imagine her sense of despair at the unfairness of her treatment.

Kate and the Spirit of
the Frontier

Kate embodied the true Frontier Spirit. Her knowledge of the land and skills passed down from generations enabled her to meet the challenges she faced and helped preserve the Tagish and Tlingit culture for future generations. She lived out the remainder of her life close to her brother Skookum Jim (Keish) near the town of Carcross.

Canadian Mining Hall of Fame

In 2019, Kate's role in the initial discovery of Gold at Bonanza creek was finally recognized and she was inducted into the Canadian Mining Hall of Fame, the first indigenous woman to be inducted.

NEWS

EIGHT PAGE EDITION

Back Before Hardships,

GOLD! GOLD! GOLD! GOLD!

MANY ENCOUNTER DANGER ON THE TRAIL

Continue the Journey

In the course of a few short years, a small number of fearless women had overcome the hardest of conditions to secure their aims of reaching the elusive gold strikes, of business success, and setting a path for freedom. History will remember them as trailblazers, paving their way for the women who followed them.

Glossary

BEDROCK
Solid rock that sits beneath loose surface material such as soil and gravel.

COLONY
An area controlled by a foreign, more powerful country.

FIRST NATION
A term to describe one of three groups who are the earliest known inhabitants of Canada.

FRONTIER
The edge or fringe of a territory.

GOLD FIELDS
An area of land where gold is found.

GOLD STANDARD
A system for linking money to the price of gold.

GOLD STRIKE
The discovery of a new source of gold.

HUMAN RIGHTS
Rights which someone possesses because they are human.

LEGAL TENDER
Anything, typically banknotes, that one is entitled to use to pay off a debt.

MINING CLAIM
A piece of land where a miner has a right to extract minerals.

OUTFIT
An essential collection of food, clothes, and tools for a miner.

PAY DIRT
Earth, gravel, or other material containing valuable minerals.

PERMAFROST
Soil, gravel, or sand permanently frozen under the ground.

STAMPEDER
Someone taking part in a gold rush.

SUMMIT
The top or peak of a hill or mountain.

TERRITORY
An area of land that is owned by a country.

TRAIL
A well-trodden off-road route

TRIBUTARIES
Streams or rivers that feed into a big river.

Sources

Berton, Pierre, *Klondike: The Last Great Gold Rush 1896-1899*, Anchor Canada, (2001)

Chaput, Don, *Nellie Cashman and the North American Mining Frontier*, Westernlore Press, (1995)

Duncan, Jennifer, *Frontier Spirit: The Brave Women of the Klondike*, Anchor Canada, (2004)

Mayer, Melanie J., *Klondike Women: True Tales of the 1897-1898 Gold Rush*, Ohio University Press, (1989)

Meissner, David, & Richardson, Kim, *Call of the Klondike: A True Gold Rush Adventure*, Calkins Creek, (2019)

Murphy, Claire Rudolf, & Haigh, Jane G., *Gold Rush Dogs*, Alaska Northwest Books, (2008)

Murphy, Claire Rudolf, & Haigh, Jane G., *Gold Rush Women*, Hillside Press, (2012)

Vanasse, Deb, *Wealth Woman: Kate Carmack and the Klondike Race for Gold*, Running Fox Books, (2016)

Whyard, Flo, *Martha Black: Her Story from the Dawson Gold Fields to the Halls of Parliament*, Alaska Northwest Books, (1998)

Wilson, Graham, *The Klondike Gold Rush: Photographs from 1896-1899*, Friday 501 Media Ltd, (1997)